DISNEP · PIXAR

a bug's life

MOUSE WORKS™

"Princess Atta!" cried Flik. "Look at this!"

Flik was an inventive worker ant, and Princess Atta was the ant of his dreams. He was always trying to impress her with his new inventions. This one was a harvesting machine.

Unfortunately Atta was too busy to pay much attention to Flik. Her mother, the Queen, was training her to rule Ant Island.

But Atta's little sister Dot thought Flik was special. She followed him as he walked away.

"Don't be sad, Flik," said Dot. "Atta always tells me I'm too little."

Flik perked up. "Hey, you're not too little," he said. "Look at this rock. Pretend it's a seed. One day it will grow into a giant tree. All it needs is time."

Dot smiled. "You're weird. But I like you," she said.

Suddenly the alarm sounded. The grasshoppers were coming!

Flik tried to follow the other ants into the anthill, but he tripped. His harvesting machine knocked over the offering stone. All the grain spilled out into a deep ravine!

"Oh, no!" cried Flik.

Just then the grasshoppers arrived. Hopper, their leader, stormed into the anthill.

"Where's my food?" he demanded. Then he picked up Princess Dot!

"Let her go!" cried Flik.

"You want her?" asked Hopper. "Go ahead—take her! But you have to collect double the amount of grain before we return!"

Then he and his gang rode off.

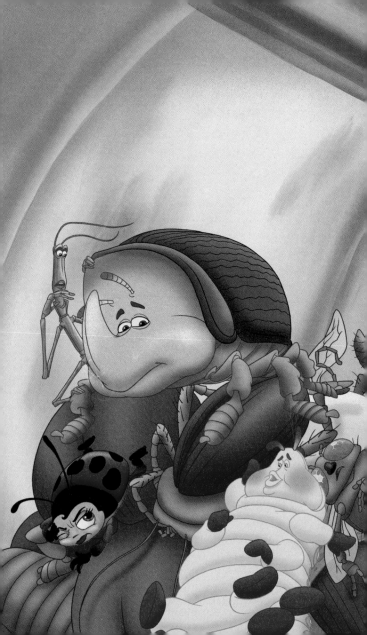

Flik felt terrible. It was all his fault that the ants were in trouble. So he volunteered to go search for bigger bugs to protect the colony from the grasshoppers.

Flik traveled to The City where he found a group of big bugs engaged in a huge brawl.

"Wow!" said Flik.

As soon as the fight was over, he asked the bugs to return to Ant Island with him. Much to his surprise, the bugs readily agreed!

Flik's return to Ant Island was triumphant. The other ants were so happy they held a special banquet to welcome the warrior bugs.

Then something happened.

As they watched the ant children enact a battle scene, the new "warrior" bugs realized the ants wanted them to fight.

"Is that us fighting?" gasped Rosie the spider. She needed to find Flik and tell him the truth—they were circus bugs, not warriors!

Flik couldn't believe it.

"Circus bugs?!" he cried as soon as they were away from the banquet.

"What in the world made you think we were warrior bugs?" asked Rosie.

Flik tried to explain, but the circus bugs were intent on leaving. As they started to fly away, Flik leaped desperately to grab them.

"Don't go!" he cried. "I'll be branded with this mistake the rest of my life!"

But suddenly Flik realized something worse was about to happen: a giant bug-eating bird appeared in the grass behind him.

"Run!" he cried.

Flik and the circus bugs raced for shelter. Just then Flik heard something.

It was Dot! She was floating on a dandelion puff with the bird chasing her!

The circus bugs knew they had to help. Along with Flik, they managed to distract the bird and rush Dot to safety.

The ants cheered loudly for their heroes.

The circus bugs were thrilled with all the applause and attention. They were, after all, performers. If the ants wanted them to be warrior bugs, they would stay and play the role—at least for now.

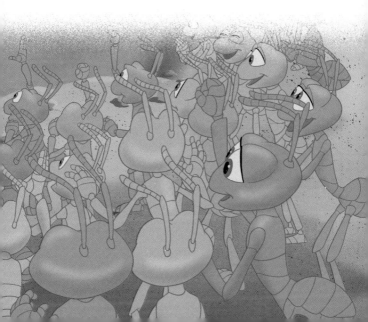

The ants and the circus bugs worked together to create a fake bird to scare away the grasshoppers. It was all Flik's idea, but he convinced the circus bugs to pretend it was theirs. He figured the ants wouldn't have a lot of faith in another one of his inventions.

On the day the bird was finished, the ant colony cheered loudly.

"Hooray!" they cried when the bird was in place. They knew they could scare away the grasshoppers for good—with the help of their fake bird...and their "warriors."

Unfortunately, later that night, Flik's whole plan fell apart. The owner of the circus arrived looking for his performers.

"You mean...you're not warriors?" Atta asked in disbelief.

Flik tried to explain, but Atta was disappointed. Flik had lied to her.

"I want you to leave, Flik," she said. "And this time, don't come back."

Dot was crushed. She begged her mother, the Queen, to let Flik stay. But it was too late. Flik and the circus bugs would have to leave Ant Island for good.

When Hopper arrived, he was furious to see how little grain there was.

"No ant sleeps until we get every scrap of food on this island!" he roared.

Not only that, but Hopper had plans to squish the Queen, too! Dot knew she had to do something. So she flew off to get Flik and the circus bugs.

"I can't help you, Dot," said Flik. "I'm just a failure."

But Dot wouldn't give up. She found a rock and handed it to Flik. "Remember what you told me about the rock growing into a great big tree?" she said.

Flik smiled. Dot was right. He had to believe in himself. The colony needed him!

Flik and the circus bugs raced back to Ant Island. Flik tried to launch the bird, but it crashed.

Gathering all his courage, Flik faced Hopper. "Ants were not meant to serve grasshoppers!" he cried.

Soon the circus bugs and the other ants joined Flik. Working together, they were able to chase away the grasshoppers for good.

The following spring, the circus bugs finally had to leave Ant Island. They were going on a new tour.

Atta, who was now queen, thanked the bugs for their help. Flik stood right next to her, and Dot was now officially wearing a princess crown.

It seemed as if everyone's greatest wish had come true at last.